P9-DCG-660

CE

Published by Reader's Digest Children's Books
Reader's Digest Road, Pleasantville, NY U.S.A.10570-7000 and
Reader's Digest Children's Publishing Limited,
The Ice House, 124-126 Walcot Street, Bath UK BA1 5BG

Manufactured in China.
Conforms to ASTM F963-03 and EN 71
10 9 8 7 6 5 4 3 2 1

Exploring with Dora

Storybook & DVD

adapted by Ruth Koeppel • illustrated by Tom Mangano

Contents

Pleasantville, New York • Montréal, Québec • Bath, United Kingdom

Daisy, la Quinceañera

Today is cousin Daisy's fifteenth birthday party! ¡La fiesta de quinceañera de Daisy!" Dora told her best friend, Boots. They were both so excited to go and dance the mambo at the party for Dora's cousin.

Just then the phone rang and Dora answered. "Happy birthday, Daisy!" she said.

"¡Gracias, prima! Don't forget to bring my special birthday crown and shoes," Daisy reminded her cousin. "I can't start the party without them."

Dora held up a pair of blue high-heeled shoes. Boots held a sparkling tiara.

"Don't worry, Daisy," Dora said. "We've got them, and we're coming! ¡Vámonos! Let's go!"

Dora packed the crown and shoes in a special box and off they went to Daisy's party.

"Remember, we need to watch out for that sneaky fox, Swiper," Dora said.

"Yeah, he'll try to swipe the box with Daisy's crown and shoes!" Boots added, holding the box tightly in his tail.

"We need to find the quickest way to Daisy's party," said Dora. "Who do we ask for help when we don't know which way to go? Map!"

Map flew out of Backpack. "To get to Daisy's party, we need to follow the path past the Barn and through the Rainforest," Map said. "That's how we get to Daisy's party!"

Dora and Boots set off toward the Barn. A big duck waddled over and started following them. "*Quack! Quack!*"

Dora and Boots saw a fox tail behind the duck.

"That's a funny-looking duck," said Boots.

It was no duck! It was Swiper! The sneaky fox reached for the box with the crown and shoes inside.

Dora and Boots yelled out, "Swiper, no swiping!"

"Oh, mannn!" Swiper said with a snap of his fingers, as he dropped the box and raced off in defeat.

Racing toward the Rainforest with the box, Dora and Boots came upon a bicycle built for two that was leaning against a tree.

"Hey, look!" said Boots. "It's Robot Bicycle!"

"Robot Bicycle can give us a ride to the Rainforest!" said Dora, as she grabbed the bike helmets from the basket.

They put on their bike helmets, hopped on the bike, and pedaled off down the bumpy path.

Suddenly, it started to rain.

"We must have made it to the Rainforest!" Dora said.

"We can't let Daisy's stuff get wet in the rain!" cried Dora. "Who might have something that can keep us dry? ¡Sí! Backpack!"

Backpack opened and an umbrella flew out to Dora.

"¡Hola, prima!" came a familiar voice. It was Diego, with Baby Jaguar.

"¡Hola, primo!" cried Dora. "We're going to your sister Daisy's fiesta de quinceañera."

"We're going, too," said Diego. "We can go together."

At that moment, a camel came out of the bushes.

"I've never heard of a camel living in the Rainforest," said Diego. "My Field Journal says camels live in sunny places, not rainy ones."

A fox head popped out of the camel. It was Swiper!

"Swiper, no swiping!" cried Dora and Boots.

"Oh, mannn!" Swiper snapped his fingers and ran off.

"We need to get to Daisy's party—quick!" said Dora.

Diego called to a pair of giant condors flying by. The condors swooped down and they all climbed on for a ride.

When they made it to the party, they saw Daisy.

Dora held out the box and said, "Happy birthday, Daisy!"

"Oh, these shoes and crown are beautiful!" said Daisy, as she gave Dora a big hug. "Now we can start the party!"

It was a good thing, as Dora and Boots were ready to do the mambo. They changed into their party clothes and joined everyone on the dance floor.

"You two are really good at dancing!" said Daisy. "Thanks for making my fiesta de quinceañera extra-special!"

Baby Jaguar's Roar

One day, Dora and Boots were visiting Dora's cousin, Diego, at the Animal Rescue Center, where there were lots and lots of baby animals.

"This is a baby spectacled bear," said Diego, as he lifted the bear so they could all see.

"He's so cute!" said Boots.

The bear pushed a ball with its nose.

"That's his favorite ball," said Diego. "Baby Bear and Baby Jaguar love to play together. They're best friends."

Baby Jaguar and Baby Bear batted the ball back and forth.

But suddenly, Baby Jaguar was jumping up and growling, "*Mreow, mreow!*"

"Uh-oh," said Diego. "Baby Bear ran off!"

Dora, Diego, Boots, and Baby Jaguar looked and looked, but Baby Bear was nowhere to be found.

"We've got to find Baby Bear!" cried Dora. "Who do we ask for help when we don't know which way to go? Yeah, Map!"

"Baby Bear ran all the way to Big Mountain!" Map told them. "To get to Big Mountain to save Baby Bear, first, we need to go through the Jungle, and then go down the Fast River—El Río Rápido...and that's how we get to Big Mountain!"

"So first, we go to the Jungle," said Dora. "¿Dónde está? Where is the Jungle?"

Baby Jaguar climbed a tree and pushed aside some leaves. Then he growled to let Diego know he had spotted it.

"Jaguars are great climbers!" said Diego. "Thanks, Baby Jaguar!"

The four explorers raced toward the Jungle.

"Hurry! Let's run like a jaguar," said Diego.

"Run, run, run!" Dora and Boots cried. "¡Corre, corre, corre!"

They ran down the road and over a hill and then to the edge of the Jungle. "We made it!" Dora cried.

"Next we go to the Fast River," said Dora. "¡El Río Rápido!"

"El Río Rápido sure is fast," said Boots, when they reached the water's edge. "How are we going to get down it?"

Baby Jaguar spotted a boat in the water and jumped in.

"Mreow, mreow!" He grabbed on to the towrope and pulled it back to Dora, Boots, and Diego.

"Yay, Baby Jaguar!" Diego cheered. "Jaguars are great swimmers!"

Dora reached in the boat and found life jackets. "¡Salvavidas! So we can be safe!" she cried, as they put on their life jackets and helmets.

Then they hopped aboard, and Diego started to paddle the boat down the Fast River.

Suddenly, a big wave came toward them.

"We've got to crouch down like jaguars!" said Dora.

They rode the wave, but foam splashed into the boat. Map popped out of Backpack's pocket and fell right into the water.

"*Whoa!*" Map cried, as he bobbed in the water.

"We've got to save Map," said Dora. "Who is a great swimmer who can save Map?"

"Baby Jaguar can do it," said Diego.

Baby Jaguar dove into the river. Baby Jaguar swam over to Map, who jumped on Baby Jaguar's back.

"Thanks, Baby Jaguar!" said Map. "*Phew!*"

Baby Jaguar swam back to the boat, and Diego reached out to help them.

"Baby Jaguar saved Map!" said Diego.

"¡Fantástico!" cried Dora.

"Good work!" agreed Boots. "*Phew!* That was really, really close."

"Sure was, Boots," said Dora. "And look!"

The boat had reached the end of the Fast River. "We made it!" said Dora. "Where do we go next?"

"Next we go to the Big Mountain to save Baby Bear!" said Map.

"Yay! We made it!" cried Dora. "Do you see Baby Bear?"

"Yeah!" said Diego. "There's Baby Bear up there!"

"But how are we going to get up there?" asked Boots.

Baby Jaguar started running and jumping up the mountain.

"We have to climb and jump like a jaguar to get up the mountain," said Diego.

They jumped over the rocks and climbed up some vines to the ledge where Baby Bear stood. But before Baby Jaguar reached the ledge, it started to crack.

"Baby Jaguar wants to warn Baby Bear," said Diego. "But he's never roared before."

"ROAR!" Dora and Boots cried.

Baby Jaguar opened his mouth wide and took a deep breath.

"ROAR!" Baby Jaguar repeated.

It worked. Baby Bear jumped onto Baby Jaguar's back, and down the mountain they went.

"*Phew!* Baby Jaguar saved Baby Bear!" Diego said. "Great work!"

Everyone high-fived, and Baby Bear nuzzled Baby Jaguar.

"We saved Baby Bear!" said Dora. "¡Lo hicimos! We did it!"

La Maestra de Música

One day, Dora and Boots were walking to school.

"I love school!" Boots said. "My music teacher always sings a special song—'The Hola, Hola Song'!"

At that moment, La Maestra rolled up on her bike to say hi to Boots.

"Maestra, this is my best friend, Dora," said Boots.

"Hola, Dora," La Maestra sang. The three of them sang "The Hola, Hola Song" together.

"Great singing, chicos!" La Maestra said, as she hopped back on her bike. "But now, I have to hurry! I have to get to school before the children do!"

Dora and Boots waved good-bye as La Maestra pedaled away. Before she'd gone very far, they heard a squeal and a crunch. Her bicycle chain had popped off.

"*Ay, yai, yai!*" said La Maestra, as she came screeching to a stop.

Boots and Dora ran over to check out the broken bike chain.

"I need to figure out the quickest way to get to school!" said La Maestra.

"Let's ask Map!" said Dora.

Map peeked out from his pocket with a big smile. "To get to school, we have to go through the Town and over Musical Mountain!" he told them.

Dora looked around. "The bus will take us to the Town," she said. "¡Pare! Stop!"

The bus skidded to a halt. Dora asked the bus if it could take them to the Town.

"¡Todos a bordo! All aboard!" announced the bus.

As La Maestra started up the bus steps, she nearly dropped a musical instrument. "I have so many instruments to carry," she sighed. "I wish I had a backpack."

Backpack lifted her flap. In went the maracas, triangles, trumpets, flutes, and bongos. Then they rode the bus through Town.

"¡Gracias, Autobus!" said Dora, when they arrived.

"De nada," said the bus.

The three passengers climbed out and headed to Musical Mountain.

"Who can give us a ride over the mountain fast?" asked Dora.

La Maestra pointed at a train.

"That's our friend Azul!" said Boots.

"¡Hola, amigos!" said Azul. Azul agreed to take them over the mountain.

"¡Vámonos!" everyone cried.

Azul chugged toward Musical Mountain, then zigzagged up the mountain path and down the other side.

"We made it over Musical Mountain!" said Dora.

Suddenly, they heard a ding-dong sound.

"That's the last bell, chicos!" said La Maestra. "We have to hurry!"

"Next we need to find the school," said Dora. "Where is the school? Oh, look, there's the school bus! The school bus is going to the school!"

"How will we catch up to it?" asked La Maestra.

Just then, Dora's cousin Diego zipped past riding a zip cord. He stopped on a platform, high in the trees.

"¡Hola, amigos!" said Diego. "Grab onto the zip cord and we'll get to school quickly!"

Dora, Boots, and La Maestra grabbed onto the zip-cord handles and zipped through the trees. Finally, Dora, Boots, Diego, and La Maestra arrived at the schoolhouse.

"*Wheee!*" said everyone. They hopped off the zip cord and ran toward the entrance.

"¡Rápido!" said La Maestra. "We have to run inside and set up the instruments for music class before the children come in!"

"Backpack!" cried Boots.

Backpack flung out the instruments. Dora caught the flute, Boots grabbed the maracas, and Diego took the trumpet.

As La Maestra's students entered, Dora, Boots, and La Maestra sang to them. La Maestra told Boots he could lead "The Hola, Hola Song."

La Maestra strummed her guitar and started to dance.

Benny, Isa, and Tico grabbed instruments from the music table and started to play along.

"Great playing, everybody," cheered La Maestra. She gave Boots a hug and he beamed proudly.

"And a special thanks to you, Dora and Boots, for helping me get to school on time!" La Maestra said.

"We did it!" cried Dora and Boots. "¡Lo hicimos!"

Star Catcher

I have a special present for you, Dora," said Abuela one day. "It is a Star Pocket for catching stars."

Boots clapped his hands. "I want to be a Star Catcher, too!"

Dora asked Backpack to wear the Star Pocket, and she was happy to do it. Abuela wished them luck.

Dora gave Abuela a hug and then turned to Boots.

"¡Vámonos! Let's go catch stars!" Dora said.

Dora and Boots made their way through the forest, looking for stars. Suddenly, the Star Pocket began to glow and swirl.

"I hear a star!" said Dora.

An Explorer Star named Woo Hoo appeared to play with Dora and Boots. Dora reached up and caught the star. Woo Hoo laughed and flew into the Star Pocket.

Dora took off her Backpack and set it on the ground. As Dora and Boots peeked into the Star Pocket, Swiper snuck up behind them.

"Swiper, no—" Dora and Boots began together.

But they were too late. Swiper swiped the Star Pocket and tied it to the string of a red balloon. The balloon floated away.

"You'll never find your Star Pocket now!" said Swiper.

"We have to get the Star Pocket back and save Woo Hoo!" said Dora.

"Where are we going to find Woo Hoo?" Boots asked Dora.

"Map!" Dora cried.

Map appeared.

"The balloon is taking Woo Hoo to the Cloud Castle!" he said. "First we have to sail across the Stormy Water, then go over Dragon Mountain, and that's how we'll get to the Cloud Castle to rescue Woo Hoo! And don't forget to try to catch stars along the way. The stars can help you save Woo Hoo!"

"So first we have to find the Stormy Water," said Dora. Along the way, Star Catcher Dora caught three Explorer stars—Saltador, Noisy Star, and Glowy. Boots also caught Switchy.

With the Explorer Stars flying overhead, Dora and Boots ran to the edge of the Stormy Water. The Explorer Stars gathered around a big ship.

"¡El barco!" said Dora.

Dora and Boots ran on deck and put on their life jackets. It got dark and stormy. The waves rose higher and rocked the boat.

Glowy flew to the front of the ship

and lit up the dark stormy seas.

"Way to go, Glowy!" cried Boots.

Suddenly, they saw sharks swimming all around them.

"What are we going to do?" asked Boots.

"Let's ask for help from our Explorer Star friends!" said Dora. "Who can help us jump over the sharks?"

"Saltador, the Super-Jumping Star!" said Dora. "He can help the boat jump. ¡Salta!"

Saltador jumped the boat over one shark after the other.

"¡Gracias, Saltador!" said Dora.

But just when they thought they were in for smooth sailing, they bumped into a sleeping whale. They couldn't get around the whale.

"We need another Explorer Star to help us!" said Dora. "Noisy Star can wake up the sleeping whale!"

Noisy Star zoomed over the sleeping whale and started to make honking sounds.

"Yay! We woke up the sleeping whale!" Boots said.

When they docked on the far shore, Dora said, "Next we go to Dragon Mountain."

The Explorer Stars made a circle around Dragon Mountain, and Dora and Boots ran over to it.

"But how are we going to get over Dragon Mountain?" asked Boots.

The stars flew over to a blue train. "Hey, that's our friend Azul," said Dora. "Azul can give us a ride over Dragon Mountain."

Soon, they were chugging up the mountain. When they reached the top, Dora said, "Look—that dragon is chasing us! ¡Vámonos! Let's go!"

Just then, Dora noticed some missing pieces in the tracks.

"Which Explorer Star can help us fill in the track?" she asked. "Switchy Star!"

Switchy changed shape and filled in the holes just in time.

The dragon flew up beside them just as Azul came to a halt.

"I was just trying to warn you about the missing pieces in the tracks," the Dragon explained. "I'm glad you got down okay."

"¡Gracias!" Dora replied. "What a friendly dragon. Okay, next we go to the Cloud Castle. It's on the highest cloud."

Saltador super-jumped them right into the castle's tower window. There they found a young prince sitting on a throne with the Star Pocket in his hands.

"Woo Hoo!" called the Baby Star, peeking out of the pocket.

"I'm the Star Catcher now!" cried the Prince. "We'll have a contest. Whoever catches the most stars can have this Star Pocket."

"Okay!" cried Dora. "Let's go!"

The Prince and Dora jumped to catch the stars, and Dora caught the most. The Prince had to admit Dora was a great Star Catcher, and he handed over the Star Pocket. Woo Hoo flew out to give his friends a big hug.

"We did it!" cried Dora and Boots. "¡Lo hicimos!"